SON of a GUN

For Erik
— *A.d.G.*

Anne de Graaf

SON of a GUN

Eerdmans Books for Young Readers

Grand Rapids, Michigan • Cambridge, U.K.

Copyright original text Anne de Graaf / Jongbloed Publishers,
Marktweg 73a, 8444 AB Heerenveen, Netherlands
Original Dutch title: *Kind van de oorlog*

This edition published 2012 in the United States of America by
Eerdmans Books for Young Readers,
an imprint of Wm. B. Eerdmans Publishing Co.
2140 Oak Industrial Dr. NE, Grand Rapids, Michigan 49505
P.O. Box 163, Cambridge CB3 9PU U.K.

www.eerdmans.com/youngreaders

The author is represented by and this book is published in association with
the literary agency of WordServe Literary Group. Ltd.,
www.wordserveliterary.com

Manufactured at Worzalla, Stevens Point, Wisconsin, USA,
in March 2012; first printing

12 13 14 15 16 17 18   8 7 6 5 4 3 2 1

Library of Congress Cataloging-in-Publication Data

De Graaf, Anne.
[Kind van de oorlog. English]
Son of a gun / by Anne de Graaf.
p. cm.
Summary: Eight-year-old Liberian Lucky, his ten-year-old sister Nopi,
and their schoolmates are kidnapped and forced to become child soldiers,
but even after they escape along with some other children and
are reunited with their parents, their lives will never be the same.
Includes chapter about Liberia.
ISBN 978-0-8028-5406-3
1. Liberia — History — Civil War, 1989-1996 — Juvenile fiction.
[1. Liberia — History — Civil War, 1989-1996 — Fiction.
2. Child soldiers — Fiction.
3. Brothers and sisters — Fiction.] I. Title.
PZ7.D33946Su 2012
[Fic] — dc23
2011032932

All photographs are by Anne de Graaf.

Prologue

I was crazy. Crazy mad. That's how I felt when I turned in my AK-47 rifle. The commanding officer's growl still haunts me: "This gun is your god. You listen to the voice of your god and go where your gun tells you." But I wanted the money, the dollars the United Nations was offering if you turned in your gun. I needed the money in order to go home, to face the future, if my past would let me.

The U.N., he came to Liberia, and now I think he's here to stay. At least I hope so. "So where do you think you're going?" Mr. Blue Helmet asked me.

I wish I knew, I thought. I watched him toss my god onto the pile of other AKs. It clattered down the side and sent up a little cloud of dust. "Won't hear no more voices from that gun," I mumbled.

He gave me the dollars; I counted them quick and shoved them deep into my crotch. Then he still wanted to shake my hand. That's cool. We snapped fingers, my third finger against his. "Where you from?" I asked.

"Ireland. What about you? Where are you from?"

"Me? I'm from Liberia, man. What you think? Ha!"

I didn't tell him the last time I went home, I found the house burned and looted. I didn't tell him this was the third time in eight years I was trying to get home. I didn't tell him about how walking has become my thing. The C.O. — that's short for commanding officer — he called them forced marches, but me, I've made it into my very own career of walking.

Part 1

Chapter 1

Nopi

Do you wonder who this boy is? This boy who is telling you this story? This boy is my brother. And me, I'm his sister. I'm two years older. He was born in 1988 and I was born in 1986. When he was still a baby the war started, near the end of 1989. The first wartime. That makes him eight years old at the beginning of this story, and I'm ten. You can call me Nopi, that's my nickname. We all have crazy nicknames here in Liberia. My brother's is Lucky. He has a gap between his two front teeth, so whenever he smiles, it makes you want to smile, too.

His favorite stories are the ones about how good it was in the old days. Or how he has heard it was. I've told my brother over and over what it was like before the war. I mean, how should I know, since those days were mostly before I was even born? But I listened to our grandma when he was too young to remember.

Listen, and let's see if you can picture this. I've heard about your side of the world, you know. Where it gets cold, and cows don't know how to swim, and there's so much food you don't even want to get fat. I wonder if there's a place for my story in your world. People say a lot of things about

Africa. Maybe you could shut out those voices now, and just listen with your heart.

If I start talking about the sun and trees pressed down by the weight of the sky and yellow grass and red dust and crickets at night and laughter and the roar of waves at the beach, can you hear Africa? Can you taste my Liberia in the salt-scented air? Can you feel the dust between your teeth? Can you hear the laughter of the children? Hey, we're just like you, you know. Well, okay, maybe a little different color, and a whole lot warmer, but you want to bet we're not afraid of the same things?

Chapter 2

Lucky

Me, this is what I remember. OK, so this is what happens. These kids are sitting in school. It's a school with walls made of sticks with mud smeared onto them, and mud bricks. The benches are rough tree trunks sawed lengthwise in half, and thin poles hold up the roof. Open windows with no glass because it's always warm, remember? We're packed into the largest room. We're having a school meeting and we're all a little scared since we heard gunshots all night. The school principal is talking to us about schedules, when suddenly, these soldiers come storming into the place in the middle of the school where we're all sitting and standing against the walls.

The girls start to scream, then stop when the soldiers point their guns at us. Man, I can tell you it was not a fine sight. I nearly wet myself I was so scared. You're laughing, but I was only eight years old.

I mean, I was just a little boy then, and all proud of myself for learning the alphabet. What did I know? The principal, Mr. Nyanforth, he walks up to the tallest soldier and he starts talking. I stand up to see better and feel my sister's hand slip over mine. She's found me in the crowd and left her friends. I look at her face and see it turn ashen, then I look back at the principal. All us kids, we jump, because the soldier takes the butt of his gun and rams it up the chin of Mr. Nyanforth and his head goes all funny and he falls down.

Then three of the teachers, all women, walk up to him. There's Mrs. Bieh. She's my teacher and even though she's really big, she has a soft voice when she reads us stories. Her hands are on her hips, which is a bad sign. Man, this soldier is going to get it for sure.

Well, what happens next, you don't want to know. I don't even know. It has something to do with a lot of hitting and more yelling. Us kids, we ran for the door. I looked real quick over my shoulder and saw all three of the teachers being pushed up against the wall and hit over and over again. All I knew is I still had my sister's hand in mine.

We ran as hard as we could, but those soldiers, they had come into our school for a reason. Not just to hurt our teachers or steal. No man, they were after us. We ran and hid in the forest, behind stacks of wood, burrowed under the brush, but when the soldiers came after us, they found us all. My sister and I hid in empty metal barrels used for storing water. I can still remember the smell of rust and how loud my breathing was inside and what it felt like to have my heart jump out of my mouth when I looked up and saw one of the soldiers looking down at me with his bloodshot eyes and stinking breath.

They grabbed us and tied us up so our hands were all connected with rope. My sister walked in front of me. It was not so nice. By now I had wet myself. So I'm wet and smelling, and we're walking in the dust. I guess you could say this was the beginning of my walking career. Walking, walking, walking.

Nopi

The rebels knew where the kids were when we had a school meeting and waited, knowing they could come and take us then. I couldn't say that to my little brother. I couldn't even think. All I knew was I had to hold onto his hand, no matter what. Where were our parents? Who were these men? Why did they bother with small, small children like us? I was only ten!

I learned later that this happens a lot, all over the world. We're called child soldiers. An AK-47 is light enough for kids to carry. And we do stuff grown-ups are too smart and afraid to try. You know what I think? I think it happens in places where they've run out of men to fight because the wars have gone on and on, and especially in countries like ours where there are diamonds or oil or something else that makes people rich and powerful. When there are no more grown-ups to fight in the wars, then they pick on us kids.

We walked a long time, and ended up in the forest somewhere near a swamp. My little brother, he kept asking where our parents were. We had heard rumors of the war getting closer. Who was fighting who? And why us?

I don't really want to talk about what happened next. I don't know if it was days or weeks, but these rebels didn't give us much to eat and hardly anything to drink, so we really depended on them for everything. I do remember that first night after the soldiers took us, my brother and I sat curled up beneath a cottonwood tree, its big roots and all the branches around us like big arms. And in the dark, while crickets screeched and big splashes sounded in the swamp, I told him his favorite stories, about how things were when we were very small, how things were when we jumped rope and danced and had more rice to eat than we knew what to do with. That's when I told him the stories our grandma used to tell us, of what it was like before the first wartime.

Chapter 3

Lucky

My sister tells me our home had electricity. We lived in the city of Monrovia and at night if you knew someone with an office in a tall building, you could go up there — she's done it with one of our uncles — climbed one of the very tall buildings in an elevator, and you could look down like you were God himself and see all the buildings sparkling in the night. Grounded stars, she called them. Me, I've never seen anything like this. She says we used to have running water, too. And a bathroom with a bathtub. I think maybe she's making some of it up, or she's remembering something Grandma told her, but it is a fact that people in Monrovia used to call it Little America, and the roads were paved, not potholed from artillery attacks.

You know Red Light? You know why that neighborhood in Monrovia is called Red Light? It's because the stoplight hanging at the intersection there used to actually turn green and yellow and red. Yeah, that was before the wars.

You know what else was before the wars found us? James and me. James was my best friend. When my counselor from the U.N. program for ex-combatants asks me what my earliest memories are, I think of James and I think of my sister.

Strange, huh? I can't see my parents from before the war anymore. I know they're out there, those memories, but I can't find them. Maybe they're not lost, just misplaced. Even when I think back to when the soldiers came to our school and dragged us off, I come up with a bunch of stuff I wish for, but nothing solid, nothing except my sister's stories.

When I was too tiny to remember, we moved out of the city and to our home in the village. That's where I met James, and he was my best friend — I said that already, right? Man, he and I did everything together. We hung out on the beach and threw rocks at the waves, wondering if we would ever see Mammie Water, a beautiful spirit woman who lives in the water and pulls people in to drown and live with her. Or maybe we would see the very tall white water spirit, called in our language, "Kupabu." He comes out of the water to eat male papaya flowers. People die of fright when they see Kupabu. Then there is also the sea leopard we call Ni-ji, which is part fish and part leopard, and lives in the sea and eats humans. Well, even though we told plenty of stories about them, we never saw any water spirits. We did see a whale once, does that count? We spent whole days doing . . . yeah, whatever it is small boys do. We helped collect firewood, that's what my sister says. We danced and bugged our sisters and helped our mothers when we had to. I think we did, anyway. Maybe the memories really are lost. Do I even want to go looking for them now? Man, no.

That same day in school Mrs. Bieh had wanted to know what our dreams were. I can remember that one. I had a dream to be a soccer player and make loads of money and listen to the crowds cheering me on as I travel the world.

But you know something? It wasn't a dream of the heart. My dream now is school and more school. It's all I want. And I know some of you all hate your teachers, and they're ugly and they stink and their nose hairs grow way too long, but man, this really is all I want. That and to be back with James playing soccer somewhere nice, or climbing a coconut tree so we can throw down a coconut and hack it open, then drink its juice, just the two of us like we used to.

Nopi

My brother's best friend came from another tribe. It was no problem before the wars found us. We all were friends and they played soccer together. I even have an aunt who married a man from a different tribe and it was no big deal. But later on, these things mattered. And James, he came from a tribe in a part of the country where there was fighting early on, which is why his parents had moved to our village.

We have two homes – the one in the village, and our grandparents' home in Monrovia city. Years later, James' uncle took him away from our home in the city, then took James out of Monrovia because their shop kept getting broken into. His uncle took him back to that part of the country where they first came from, before he moved to our village and met me and Lucky. I'll never forget that day five years later, after the war, when both James and Lucky had become men and Lucky saw James for the last time. Lucky stood on the road and watched him go, then squatted down and sat in the dust, drawing with some stick the rest of the day. Ma sent me out to go get him in the evening. It was time for rice, and he never missed his rice. A Liberian hasn't eaten that day unless there's been rice on his plate. That's what our grandma used to tell us. Anyway, we never heard Lucky say another word about James after that. But that was after. Long after all of this. In the beginning, James was with us.

What do you want to know? You're probably still hanging back there with the soldiers, wondering what happened after that first night, am I right? Well, you think this is going to be a miserable story, I bet. You think, *Oh no, more bad stuff from Africa.* Well, we have a surprise for you, me and my brother. So hold on for the ride.

I'll take you back to that day — no, even better, I'll take you back to that night. It took a long time, that night, and all I could think of was my little brother and how scared he was. That's not true — I also kept thinking about our parents. You see, the soldiers had been coming closer and closer to our village. You mixed up yet? Why weren't we in the city? Well, we used to live there, and I really can remember the lights in the city. But then the war started, and we moved to the country like a lot of other people. We kept thinking the war would be over soon and we could move back home. The soldiers coming to our school that day when I was ten, that was something no one thought would ever happen. Well, no one thought we'd get stuck in the middle of fourteen total years of war either.

Of all my memories, that first night away from home, away from school, away from our parents, that one won't go away no matter how often I tell it to get lost.

Chapter 4

Lucky

They untied us and took the girls away somewhere else. I sat with the other little boys and it was real hard not to cry. When the sun finally came up I found myself waking because someone's foot kept tapping my shoulder. It was a big boy from the older classes. He was kicking me under that tree while he slept, just like a dog sometimes does. The soldiers came and lined us all up and told us that we would become soldiers now. If we listened real good, we would be rewarded with food and water. If we learned real fast, we could get our own guns and make sure no one ever hurt us again.

"Listen up!" The sergeant bellowed like a big bull. He even shook his head back and forth and shuffled his right foot like it was a hoof and he was getting ready to charge at us. This was Sergeant Saint. "You say 'Yes sir' and 'No sir' to everything. You follow orders and you'll get more than just food and water, you'll get money and loot. But first you have to earn your way and carry these bags of rice and millet, understand?"

The big boy who woke me that morning with his foot stepped out of line and said, "You can't just kidnap us like that and expect us to work for you . . ." But no sooner were the words out of his mouth than Sergeant Saint shot him dead, right there in front of us. I had never seen anyone shot dead like that before. And it rips something right out of your heart to see the life leave a body.

Then I heard others making noise, screaming and crying all around me. It took me a few minutes to realize some of the noise was being made by me. Sergeant Saint walked right up to me and raised his hand. I saw it block out the sun and I saw the diamond ring on his smallest finger catch the light. It shone like fire as it came down fast.

The blow drove me to my knees. For some strange reason I looked up and just couldn't stop watching Sergeant Saint's face twist even uglier. I smelled the wood smoke from the cooking fires, heard my classmates howling, felt tears drop onto my neck, and tasted salt and dust on dry lips.

"No! Lucky, get down! No!" I looked to the right and saw Nopi running like a wild girl. I had found my sister. She looked different. I couldn't believe how fast she ran. There I was, kneeling in the dust, barely able to turn my head, and there she was racing like lightning across the sky. She tackled Sergeant Saint — well, not really, I mean she threw herself at him.

Boom! She slammed right into him. And he started to laugh. It was this awful sound like walking in mud, a sucking sound that pulled me in and made me scared. The slow-motion feeling stopped and I held my breath. My chest felt like it would burst. I gasped. Now it was my turn to scream, "No!"

The sergeant leaned over and picked Nopi up by her hair. Even then she fought, kicking in the air at him. His laugh grew in volume until it shook us all like thunder. I found a hand slip into mine and pull me to my feet. I looked at the owner of the hand. It was James. He squeezed my hand.

The next instant I saw that diamond ring catch the light again, and this time it landed on the side of Nopi's face. Sergeant Saint flung Nopi down onto the ground and her head landed so the other side of her face hit a rock. Then he kicked her in the ear with his boot and walked away from us.

James let me go and I ran to her. Nopi's school uniform skirt had blood stains on it, but now blood from her ear bubbled out and ran onto her white collar. I was thinking about how the life had just crept out of the big boy's body. Would the same thing happen to Nopi? I waited, then touched her face. Nopi's face is heart-shaped, and she likes to wear colorful scarves woven through her hair. Her favorite is bright orange, and she wore that one at school the day before, but it had gone in the night. Her eyes are big and dark and go right through you when she's angry. I couldn't see her eyes now. She just lay there, not moving. I waited some more. I heard nothing but my heart beating loud as the world stopped turning. I waited.

Nopi

Music! Music ran all around me and through me like water. Or I was water and ran all around and through the music. But it was music without a beat, more like music I could breathe.

Then I felt Lucky's fingers on my cheek. I opened my eyes and the music stopped. I could see his mouth open wide and I felt his hand squeezing my arm. I reached up to touch the blood dripping off his other hand. Where was he hurt? I wondered.

My head began to ache, then pain shot through me from the top down, filling all the same places the music had just been, and I remembered. I remembered. And I forgot. I didn't want to remember.

Lucky pulled me up so I could sit, and James came up behind Lucky and opened his mouth wide too. Both boys had tears streaming down their faces. Why were they making such funny shapes with their mouths?

And then I had to remember, and with that memory came understanding. I put a hand up to touch my ear and felt warm blood. I looked down as it caked my shoulder. It felt like someone had stuck a knife through my head, in one ear and out the other. I opened my mouth and felt my throat open and close, but I heard nothing. I heard nothing! Not my voice, not the cries of the boys beside me, not the birds in the trees, nothing!

Later I would think about this moment in my life and realize many things had happened. The kick. The landing on the rock. The fist with the ring. All these things added up to one. What is this one? A silence that will not let me go. A silence that grips me and follows me in and out of sleep. A silence worse than anything I had ever known before, worse even than the pain that ground in and out of my head until many days later, when the bleeding finally stopped and the bruises faded away.

Part 2

Chapter 5

Lucky

My sister is deaf because of me. This thought waited for me every day like a lion waiting for its prey.

I don't know how many days went by. When I look back at them now, they run together. I see myself walking and carrying heavy sacks of grain and jerry cans of water. I am thirsty all the time. James and I no longer talk about soccer. We do not argue about AC Milan and Real Madrid. We stay very close to each other and talk about school. We name our teachers and we recite the alphabet to each other because that was what we were learning when the soldiers came and kidnapped us.

The first days were the hardest because so much of my body hurt: my stomach from the emptiness, my feet from the stones I trip over, my knees from falling down too often, and my arms from carrying and dragging the heavy sack they give me every morning. But worst of all is the ache in my heart about Nopi.

I see her often. They do not really separate us well. There is a group of boys and a group of girls, but when we are walking through the forest, we can easily come alongside each other.

Nopi's voice changes into words with no feeling. My sister is so smart, she is figuring out how to read my lips. But I see confusion written across her face most of the time. I watch her watching others and copying them, so I know this is her way of hearing now.

Where do we go? Where are we? Who are we? Alone in the world. Where am I going?

There are days with nothing happening. We sleep during the day and the soldiers go out to kill and attack during the night. There are nights with nothing happening, too. I don't know who the enemy is until years later when the cause of this war is explained to me. But at that time, as a small small boy, I only think about me, Nopi, and James.

The worst is when there is the killing of the stragglers. You would think that I could get used to the killing. Well, I did eventually, but not yet. And every day the children who lagged behind would get yelled at and beaten by Sergeant Saint or one of the other soldiers. After many days, some of them lay in the dust and could not stand up. Then one of the big boys would get a machete or cutlass shoved into his hands as the Sergeant bellowed, "Kill him, or you'll be killed yourself."

They called this target practice.

Nopi

This morning I asked, "What's next?" I looked up and saw my brother bringing me a cup of something warm. I saw his old-man eyes in a small boy's face, his trying-to-be-a-smile mouth, and his long fingers around the mug. Where did he find the mug? I wondered. How did he make the fire and warm the water? The water was colored green from the leaves he had boiled. This cup of tea made me cry. I felt the sounds come up out of my throat, and said the words, "Thank you, little brother."

He nodded and pursed his lips together like it was a normal thing that we should find ourselves in such a place, in the forest, surrounded by sleeping children as soldiers patrolled and the sun peeked over the edge of the horizon and entered between the high tree branches.

"Don't ever tell them I can't hear," I said to him.

"Are you sure you can't?" his lips made the shapes carefully. I had already taught him that whenever he was with me, he should make sure he faced me and spoke slowly.

I watch more than I used to when I could hear. I watch a small group of older boys whisper together and look carefully over their shoulders. But now I can understand what they say to each other. I can see their lips move and I know that they're planning to escape. The boy with the long hair tied up with a red bandana, he is the leader, and he's said several times that he knows this part of the forest, and he knows the way back to Monrovia.

This is my plan. If Lucky and I can go with them, then we can find our village on that road to Monrovia. Red Bandana knows the countryside. We could escape on our own, but we don't know the swamp and I'm afraid the forest would swallow us.

So I cross the clearing to these boys and I say to them that I know their plans. I know and they must take me and my brother.

Their lips say, "We don't want to take a girl and a small

boy. You will slow us down."

I say, "I see things. How did I know what you were talking about, huh? You need us. We are small, but we are smart. My parents have food. When we reach them, you can rest and eat and then go on to Monrovia. Take us with you, please."

Their eyes said, "No." But before I would let that thought reach their mouths, I said, "I will do anything to go with you. What do you need?"

Red Bandana nodded. "Little sister, you are brave. We need a gun. You get us a gun and you can come with your brother. This is fair?" He looked at the others and they looked at their feet. I knew what they were thinking.

No way could a girl get a gun.

Chapter 6

Lucky

I don't think anyone noticed that Nopi was deaf because our hearts were so full of listening to the voices of our own pain. So she told me not to say anything and I didn't.

Then one night she found me and shook my shoulder, and we stole away into the dark after the soldiers had been drinking. They drank to celebrate a great battle they won that night. They came back and drank. But I am telling this part of our story all wrong, backward instead of forward. Let me start with that day, when we struck camp after walking all night. We slept under the trees, closing our eyes as the crickets who sing all night finally grew quiet. Maybe they were going to sleep, too.

I woke in the evening, to sounds of shouts and gunshots. Our enemy had followed us during the day and caught up with us as we slept. The soldiers ran through the camp shouting orders. We were under attack! I heard the shots coming from behind the trees and when I looked to see where they struck, I saw men falling to the ground like birds from the sky.

No one checked now to make sure the boys and girls stayed separated. James and Nopi and I always tried to keep track of each other for moments like this when no one was looking. And sure enough, we came together and crouched behind a cottonwood tree.

Sergeant Saint's wide nose flared like it might fly right off his face. "Get out here! All of you, report for duty!" I knew what this meant. We had been through this so many times in the past. If we didn't stand in front of him in a line, the others who did would be sent to find the rest and he would make them hit the ones trying to hide. I didn't want to be hit. But even worse, I didn't want to be the one who did the hitting, so I hoped everyone would get into line.

He herded us into a part of camp that didn't seem to be under attack. "Listen closely. I'll give you all guns and you can keep them if you'll run that way," he pointed toward the trees where the gunshots kept blasting from. "Run that way and shoot the enemy. Then you can keep your guns!"

We looked at each other. He was giving us a choice? I don't know if I was old enough to realize that, but looking back and telling this story to you, I can see that this is true. It was the first time we had a choice. Well, I knew what my choice was. I looked down at my toes wiggling in the dust like fat worms. A funny thought hit me then. I wished the big boys hadn't stolen my shoes earlier. It would have felt better to be wearing shoes at a time like this.

None of us stepped forward to claim the guns Sergeant Saint offered. He just stood there, his arms bristling with a bouquet of guns pointing every which way.

I heard a voice say, "I will go." I looked up and stepped out of line to see who had said it. All us small boys looked at each other. Who was this? And as I asked the question, the voice spoke again, this time more loudly, and I knew who it was.

Nopi stepped out from among the boys. "Give me a gun," she said in her funny voice that didn't go up and down anymore. She walked right up to Sergeant Saint like he was a mountain and she had crossed a desert to reach him.

She grabbed one of the guns, pulled it out of the stack in his arms, turned, and ran screaming into the trees where the enemy soldiers still shot at us. But as she ran, the enemy fired artillery and it hit the ground and rocked us so we had to fall into the dust and crawl away from the attacks. I watched Nopi. She didn't get hit; she dropped to the ground too, with explosives falling all around her. She crawled like a snake, zigzagging across the open area until she reached the forest. Then I saw her stand and run.

"Man, she's fearless," James said.

I took a good look around and noticed even Sergeant Saint wasn't too sure about running toward those trees. Some of the soldiers were following orders, but most of the officers hung back.

Time has a funny way of working at moments like this. I had time to see that no one else wanted to go into the forest. I knew I didn't want to, but I knew I had to. I knew Nopi had done something that would get her killed. I didn't know why she did it. I just kept looking and thinking and before I could get my feet to move in her direction, the shelling stopped. The bullets stopped.

The officer in charge of Sergeant Saint came out of the trees with his men. These were the crack troops, big men we looked up to and hoped we might live long enough to fight like. "Fierce noise," one of them said.

"Couldn't hear myself think," the other said.

Then I started running. It was like a motor in me just kicked over. I ran toward them, ran past them, into the forest. Bodies and pieces of bodies lay scattered on the plants and at the foot of trees. Charred holes gaped where the grenades had fallen. I looked up and saw Nopi walking toward me. I ran up to her. "Nopi! You are so stupid! What if you died?"

"I'm not stupid," she said in her funny voice. "I didn't hear any of the noise. And we need this gun to get out of here."

Then she told me her plan.

Nopi

If I had known what waited for me in the forest, I wouldn't have run in so fast where others hesitated. I saw them holding their ears and thought, It's only sound. I was a foolish child.

I knew we were in a war, a war where children must leave their childhood behind. I knew these things, but in my pride, I thought the war would not touch me.

I thought not hearing meant not feeling the fear when I entered the dark space under those trees, not smelling smoke and sweat and spilled blood, not tasting the metal bitterness of fear as my mouth went dry and I could no longer swallow.

I fell to the ground, but one of the soldiers with wild red eyes hauled me to my feet. He pointed at dark shapes moving in the shadows and mouthed something at me. He put his hands over mine, placed them properly onto the trigger and the butt of the gun, aimed, and shot.

The next thing I knew, his hands were gone and I was shooting on my own. I ran forward, spraying the trees with bullets. I looked behind me once and saw this same soldier, the touch of whose fingers still gripped mine, lying in the dust. I looked forward and saw our men fighting off the enemy, then I staggered out into the light to find my brother.

Some things you lose and forget about. Other things walk after you every day of your life, but never quite find you again. I've felt like the child I was is still stuck in that forest, walking and walking, as I used to walk and walk.

I know I've left that little girl behind and she'll never find me again.

Chapter 7

Nopi

Red Bandana was true to his word. When I brought him the gun that night he even let me bring James and Lucky and wouldn't let any of the other boys say anything. He told me to wait until the soldiers were good and drunk. Then we all left the camp and it was so easy, compared to marching at night and being afraid Sergeant Saint or one of his men would hurt us.

For days and days we walked and crept and picked our way through the forest until we found a path. This path led to a dirt road. And the road led to a paved highway. It took so many days I lost count. We ate the large cooking bananas called plantains whenever we found them ripe. Sometimes we ate bush yams or palm cabbage, and every now and then we got to suck on sugar cane. We scrounged whatever we could find in the forest.

Finally the day came when I recognized the way the trees lined a curve in the road. "I think we're close," I said to Lucky. He didn't look so good, so tired, dragging his feet. James walked with his arm around Lucky, but I think they held each other up. We didn't talk much during the walking. It took all our strength to keep up with Red Bandana and the older boys.

We turned the curve and what I saw stopped me cold: the path leading into the forest toward our village. I recognized it because of the little stream and the giant tree trunk.

"Yes, this is it! This is it!" I thanked Red Bandana and so did James and Lucky. We headed into the forest on the path leading home. Now James and Lucky didn't lean on each other any more. I turned only once to wave and watch Red Bandana and the other older boys as they continued on the paved road to Monrovia.

Lucky

So I'm thinking, now this nightmare is over. James and I can get back to normal.

And normal means soccer. I'm a fan of AC Milan. James likes Real Madrid. I was born to be a midfielder. Man, there is nothing better than running down the field, James at my left, warding off the other team, alone with the ball and knowing my foot will send it straight into the goal.

As I ran down that path toward our village, I felt like I was just about to score. I thought, finally our walking is over. But even before we reached our village, at the place where the stream joins the path, I saw something was wrong. Someone had left a cooking pot behind. It sat rolled over on its side. I pushed it upright and saw it had no holes, so why would anyone leave a perfectly good cooking pot behind?

James said, "There's no laundry on the rocks."

It was true. No women by the water and no laundry drying on the grass or nearby rocks. In fact, it was very quiet — too quiet.

I looked up and saw Nopi running toward home. I scrambled back up the bank and ran after her, James and I racing now. Nopi went around the last bend, then I heard her funny voice cry out like an animal's.

Now I stopped. I didn't want to go any farther, but something pulled me and then I saw our village burned. Burned and looted. Fire had eaten the homes and all that stood now were a few frames and some pieces of thatch. Black charred marks showed us where the worst of the fire had raged. I walked up to Nopi. She stood in the place where our home used to stand. It was made of thatch and mud bricks, but now you couldn't have known that. It was just a heap of nothing, some piles of mud bricks, some grass, a piece of cardboard.

I could hear James crying and went over to him. My friend, my best friend, stooped before his own hut, half of which still stood upright, and he pointed inside. I looked and saw bodies lying stacked against the wall like firewood.

I pulled James away from there. We went back to the stream and sat waiting for Nopi. James finally stopped crying and picked up rocks and threw them as far as he could. I joined him, but he threw the farthest. Every now and then I looked over and saw his face, the tears still streaming like the water at our feet.

Chapter 8

Nopi

The worst part was I didn't know what had happened. I felt sorry for James, losing both his parents. I felt so sorry for him I thought my heart would break. Such a little boy to lose something so big. But then, when are we ever big enough to lose our parents?

Where could we go? What should I do? These questions grabbed me now and shook me all over as I walked back down the path and saw the boys throwing rocks.

And then, I just knew. I called to them, "Come on, James! Lucky!"

They looked up at me, their eyes all wide with fear. It was like we knew this was worse than when we were with the soldiers. Now there was no dream anymore of coming home to the village.

We would have to dream of something else. But I already knew what it looked like, this dream. "We're going to Monrovia. I'm sure they're at our old house in the city. Come on!" I kept walking. At first they didn't join me, but once I hit the big road, both boys were walking at my side again.

Lucky

You don't want to hear about the road to Monrovia. I kept hoping we would catch up with Red Bandana, but we didn't. I just added this to all my other walking experiences. It was long and hot and dry. Days and nights of walking and eating whatever we came across. The closer we came to the city, the more people we ran into. When I could see the bridge and beyond that, all the burned-up houses and streetside stands and stores, I heard someone say, "They think the war may be over soon. Man, I can't believe we made it!"

When I told Nopi, she smiled, but didn't jump up and down like I thought she would. James just looked at me when I told him. He had dead eyes now, maybe dead from all the walking, maybe dead from seeing his parents like that. I shook my head. The house we headed for actually belonged to my grandparents. Nopi and I were born there, but we had moved out of the city when things got rough. Our father had said we would be safer in the village than in the city.

As we started passing big buildings, I could see he was right. The city looked worse than our village. Huge chunks of concrete lay in strange places, and apartment buildings had lost whole walls so you could look right inside people's living rooms. Most of the traffic headed the same way we did, toward the city. There weren't many cars; it was just one long line of people, a lot of them pushing wheelbarrows with clothes and jerry cans inside. Some had things on their heads, but most were just like James, Nopi, and me.

We had nothing.

Chapter 9

Nopi

I didn't know where I was going. I just followed the road. And it was strange now to be back in a place I could remember because we lived there when I was small, but to remember it with noise, and now see it in silence.

No signs showed me to our grandparents' place. My feet found it anyway. It's a stone house on the beach. To see the ocean again, but not hear it, I felt cheated. But none of this would matter if I could just see our parents and get rid of the awful feeling I had been carrying around with me since I watched Red Bandana walk off. I think this awful feeling was knowing I was the only one around to take care of Lucky and James.

The boys could hardly walk. How could I care for them? I pushed the thought aside. Where was the house? Had we passed it? Everything looked so different now because of the rubble and broken bricks.

Then I saw it. And I saw something else. I saw people standing around in the yard. I wanted to run, like I had so many days earlier at our village, but my feet wouldn't take me. I raised my chin and opened my mouth and felt the cry come out of my heart. "Ma! Pa! Ma!"

The people turned to look at me, their backs changing to faces, and I saw them! I saw my parents! They ran toward us with arms outstretched and my other aunties and their husbands and the neighbors of my grandparents and my old grandma even, they all ran toward us.

I stood then, too tired to take another step. James stood on one side of me and Lucky on the other.

Lucky

"There they are!"

"Lucky!"

"Thank you, sweet Jesus!"

"Nopi!"

Voices and shouts and laughter and tears. I forgot about my stomach and the walking career. I even forgot about James' parents. We hugged and danced and laughed and ate rice. The war was over!

Chapter 10

Lucky

I wish to speak of the expectation of something good, then hope all broken up.

Sometimes you want a story to finish. "Stop the story right here, please," you say, as if it were a bus and you want to get out at this place. But this is real life and none of what I tell here is made up, so a bus is the wrong picture to have in your mind. Think instead about your own heart and all that is precious to you. What do you carry in your heart?

I carry hope in mine. You have entered my world and found the courage to not walk away. Stay with me now, for the heart of this story is about to be revealed. What happens to hope all broken up? Does it scatter to the sea? Or does it sow seeds too small to notice at first?

Our father was a treasure hunter, a diamond searcher. Sometimes he told us stories about going to search in the rivers of Lofa, in another part of Liberia. He told how he helped dig in the mud and loaded pebbles and mud into baskets and dumped it into sifters. Our father would hold his square sieve up to the sky, waiting for the sun to catch the light of rough diamonds. He shook it in circles as the mud and water fell to the ground below. Always he watched for the stones that caught the light. This is how he told the story, and I could see it clearly in my mind, as if I sat and watched him from a rock. I felt proud when he said that the other men followed whenever he moved up or down the river. This meant they seemed to think my Pa knew better than anyone else where to look for the diamonds.

"It is a blessing and a curse," our mother told us. "A fever that will not leave your father's blood."

"From this 'curse' we will have enough to pay your school fees," Pa said. I looked at Ma, but she wasn't mad. She nodded and smiled at us.

I think our father must be the best diamond finder around. Before the war he was gone for weeks at a time. After the war he had a hard time finding work. I knew this because he stayed home with us, fixing up the house after the damage done to it by looters during the war.

Nopi

I wish now I didn't kill those men in the forest. The war was probably already over and we would have gone home anyway. Why did I do such a foolish thing? Now I have blood on my hands. God will never forgive me. If my parents knew, they could never forgive me. I see Lucky waiting for me to tell our parents, but I can't bring the memory back by putting words into my mouth. I choke on the memory and the words would kill me . . . as I deserve.

We eat rice every day now. Our family is complete and I thank God for this. But I'm different, and so is little Lucky. He wets his bed and cries out at night. I know this because I see our mother come and hold him and take him onto my parents' sleeping mat in the late night hours.

I still can't hear anything. I continue to watch people's lips. Lucky says everyone talks louder when they want to say something to me. What I wish is that they would turn their heads and face me, that makes it easier to guess what they're trying to say.

A friend of Pa's knows a doctor and I went to him. He said if I could get to a good hospital, they might be able to operate and I'd hear again. When would this happen? How? Who would pay? Who cares for a girl who is a secret killer?

In this time of peace, I have become an old woman in a young girl's body.

Chapter 11

Lucky

We'd been home for many weeks, many months. There was still no school, but except for the ruined buildings and no running water or electricity, it was like there had never been a war.

In town one day I heard of men looking for people to hire who knew how to work in diamond rivers. "My Pa!" I ran up to them and tugged on their shirts. "My father's the best one at this." Then I ran home to tell my parents how I'd helped them. And I had told the men where we lived. They would come see my father that evening. I wanted my parents to be impressed that their almost-ten-year-old son could bring in this sort of business contact.

Instead, I saw them frown. "You should not talk so much to strangers," my grandma said from where she sat in a corner.

My grandma always praised me, so this was a blow to hear her words in this way.

"But they're searching for diamond diggers," I said, looking from one adult face to the next. No one was happy with me, that was clear. Now that James had left Monrovia with his uncle, there was no one for me to run to and play with. James lived with us for a short while until his uncle came and claimed him. Then Ma told me that the shop of James' uncle kept getting broken into, so he took James back to the part of the country where he originally came from. Without James there was nothing to do. With the grown-ups mad at me I didn't want to stay in the house, so I found Nopi down by the beach, doing laundry.

I sat and watched the surf, listening to the booming waves farther up the beach. Was it true that spirits lived in the sea and pulled you under to take you to their homes on the other side? I fell asleep in the afternoon sun.

When I woke, it was to the sound of gunshots. I must be dreaming, I thought. I sat up and saw Nopi packing up the laundry into her plastic tub. She placed it on her head and started walking toward home.

I dashed after her and touched her arm. She turned to smile at me. "So you woke up?" she asked.

"Gunshots!" I said. Her smile melted and now she gripped me back, her fingers digging into my arm.

"Where?"

"Near our house!"

She didn't wait to watch my face any longer, but started running home. I didn't have to steady a basket on my head, so I ran faster. I heard no more gunshots on the way. While I ran, an old fear snuck up behind and grabbed me.

Nopi

The first thing I saw when I ran up to our house was Ma's yellow skirt.

It had begun to rain, the great clouds and lightning

rolling in from across the sea. Rain pelted us and we could only stand there outside our house, neither of us daring to enter. I knew Lucky waited for me to go in first. I didn't want to.

My mother's yellow skirt lay in the mud by the tree like a warning. What did that mean?

The door of our house hung off its hinges. I crossed the yard and walked through the door. I could already see something terrible had happened. The sleeping mats and clothing and cooking pots lay scattered in no order throughout the room. Someone had come here and stolen from us. Thieves. But then why was the rice still in its container? And where were Ma and Grandma and Pa?

I looked at Lucky and knew I had to keep him busy. He had a wild wide look in his eyes. "They'll be back," I said. "Ma, Grandma, Pa, they probably went to report the theft."

Chapter 12

Lucky

Even I didn't believe my sister's words.

So that night as we waited for our family to return to us, I listened to the sound the rain made, like rocks pummeling the metal roof of our home. I listened and I knew what had happened. The men I told about Pa being the best diamond sifter, these men must have come and taken him and Ma away. And Grandma?

This was my fault then. My fault. Just like when Nopi became deaf. My fault. If I hadn't been bragging about Pa, we would all still be safe. The men probably came here looking for uncut diamonds. Sometimes the sifters keep the best diamonds for themselves. But we have none. There is no hiding place, that's what Pa said. Everything my father found he turned in to his employers. I think.

The more I looked at what had happened, the more I realized there must be diamonds somewhere in our house. That's what I would do if I were a great diamond sifter like Pa. I would make sure there was a little treasure for the family. But maybe there was, and the men had found it and taken it with them, which was why they left the rice behind.

These thoughts went through my mind like a vulture

that keeps circling the same place over and over, some-times lower, sometimes higher, but never landing on anything solid.

Then, in the middle of the night we heard explosions and ran outside. The blasts came from the city center. We could see great lights, then darkness. "It must be artillery fire," I said.

Nopi didn't hear me.

Part 3

Chapter 13

Nopi

A neighbor came to our house this morning. "War has broken out again," she said, hanging her head.

"Did you see what happened here yesterday?" I asked her.

She shook her head and gave me the strange look people do when they hear my voice. I must be talking differently now that I no longer hear what I say.

"The war is spreading."

She talked about the war as if it were a disease.

Lucky

"Who's doing the fighting?" I asked our neighbor.

"Soldiers."

"But which soldiers?"

"Government soldiers and rebel soldiers. The rebels are from the north part of Liberia."

It would be a long time before I understood that this war was different from what happened almost a year earlier. Different names for the groups of soldiers — same reasons of power grabbing and same greed for diamonds — same death and confusion.

Two nights later soldiers came to our part of the city, searching houses for loot. I saw them leave the neighbor's house with sacks of rice and boxes while the neighbor stood outside crying.

I knew our house would be next.

Nopi

I can't do this again. I can't have them do to me what they did before. I don't care which soldiers they are, government or rebel.

Lucky

I hid my sister in the cupboard. When the soldiers came to our house, they liked that it had two extra rooms and said they would be sleeping here. They ate our food and made me run errands for them the first few days. They had someone with them who could cook, so I got to eat after the soldiers did. They made a mess of Ma's walls and floor. What would she say when she came home and saw?

At night when the soldiers were snoring I snuck some cooked rice to Nopi. I don't know how she survived like that, day after day. Late at night she would creep out and stretch her legs a little, but we didn't want to leave since our parents might come back any day.

I fed her like this for a week, hiding her from the soldiers. Then one night the soldiers brought whiskey and beer with them. They talked about a hotel they had attacked. They became drunk, and I became afraid as they pushed me around and made me do things for them, laughing, with wild red eyes like the soldiers who took us into the forest.

Chapter 14

Nopi

I can't hear what happens in the house. I feel the thuds of the soldiers' boots, though. And I smell them; their sweaty stink comes through the cupboard door. I smell the wood fire from outside when their cook makes meals. Until now, no one has opened the cupboard door. I've hidden here for nearly a week. There's a crack and a section of uneven wood, so I can see shapes moving around the room. Light darkens as someone passes, then returns after they're gone.

I worry about Lucky. Tonight the soldiers drink too much and are dancing with Lucky. I can't see much, but it's more than I can hear. When it's very late the moon casts its light across the opening. This is usually when Lucky brings me my water and food and I step out and empty my bucket. But tonight he doesn't come.

I wait another day and night, feeling the soldiers' boots as they get up late the next morning. Finally they go somewhere else and Lucky opens the cupboard for me. I can barely stand up now. But when I do, I see bruises on his arms and a gash across his chin. Even worse, I see in his eyes a new hardness and recognize something from myself.

The little boy has fled forever.

Lucky

I told Nopi, "We're going. Tonight. Before they get back. Now."

She hesitated, then nodded. "This is no way to live," she said. I didn't know if she meant her hiding in a cupboard, or my being hurt by the soldiers.

I didn't want to leave without something from our parents. So I took my grandma's cane that she always took everywhere with her. Now at least I could hit anyone who tried to attack us.

Nopi packed some food and we ran away from the city.

We dove into the forest and followed a path parallel with the big main road.

I didn't ask her where we were going, and she didn't ask me. It was like we walked back in time and had never left the war, never found our family, never been safe.

After some time I told her we had to stop and rest. It would soon be light, so we walked deeper into the rainforest and found a tree with wide branches. We climbed up into it and stretched out on our bellies like leopards do.

"You can sleep like this?" I asked her.

But she couldn't hear me and wasn't facing my direction. I watched her lay her head down onto the moss. I did the same, but didn't think I'd ever sleep again.

Chapter 15

Lucky

Running and hiding, running and hiding. The soldiers move during the day, so we move at night. The soldiers fight at night, so we hide and move by day. I never knew a forest could be so small. No sooner do we find a place with some water and a few bananas, and soldiers march through our clearing. Nopi may not be able to hear, but she can tell when soldiers approach. She lies down in the mud and puts her head next to a rock. So many times she looks up at me and nods. Then we hide again.

I don't know how long we lived off the forest like that. Then one night I heard children's voices and headed for the sound. I found a small campfire with children even younger than us, and some teenagers. By now I was ten. I knew I had had a birthday, since my parents had been getting me excited about it when we all were still together. So surely that day had already come and gone.

My age was two numbers, so I would get to eat two chickens, that's what Grandma had said.

These other children were from the city and from villages. They had been like us, traveling in small groups until they stumbled on bigger groups. I was glad to see them.

Maybe the older ones could help us.

Nopi and I decided it would be safer to join them, even though some of the boys looked even wilder than I felt, their hair all in knots and matted together. We weren't really trying to go anywhere. We just wanted to stay away from the soldiers.

One night someone started talking about soccer.

"I want to be a soccer star," I said.

Others nodded and said, yeah, so did they.

"Our family has cousins in America. Maybe after the war I'll go there," the tall boy said.

"America! My uncle says they had their ships with Marines anchored off the coast of Monrovia when this war broke out. How come they sat offshore and waited when the shooting started? How come we have to go through another war? Why didn't the ship send Marines in to stop the killing?"

"Both the rebels and government soldiers want diamonds," I said.

"Yeah. And they want to control the government."

"All politicians just want more money and power." That's what my Pa used to say.

Nopi spoke up. "I want to be president." I was glad she couldn't hear the others laugh at her.

Nopi

I don't hear what they say. I watch their mouths, but Lucky is the only one who makes sure he faces me when he speaks. If I don't see their lips, I don't know what they say. Every now and then I say, "Yeah," or "Man," but no one listens to me. These are mostly boys. There is one other girl. She is very small, maybe six. And I become her ma, caring for her, holding her and drying her tears. The boys leave me alone. I think they are glad there is someone who knows how to cook now. I show them what to look for in the forest and soon they are all good at bringing in palm nuts for oil, or cassava to be cooked for the meal at night.

I don't know how long we ran and hid — weeks? Months? And then one day all our wandering led us right up to the front line. Of course, we wouldn't have gone there if we'd known. But the government soldiers on one side and the rebels on the other were all sleeping when we entered this area. We found a few trees and climbed them to sleep after walking all day. At night the soldiers woke and started shooting at each other. Where do you think we were? Right in the middle! It was hard to know who was who. The soldiers wore different things. A lot of the rebels wore bits of military uniforms they had stolen off dead government soldiers, or local costumes and their charms, so you couldn't tell who was who by what they wore. The rebels braided their hair in long cornrows.

Bombs and grenades exploded all around us. The shaking tree is what woke me. I slid down my tree and looked around for Lucky.

Lucky

I called to her. We heard the soldiers enter the clearing. The other children and me, we woke and slipped down, out of the branches into the bush to run away.

I called to Nopi, but of course she didn't hear. Why didn't I sleep in the same tree? Why didn't I run back and climb up to shake her shoulder and wake her? Why didn't I throw a rock at her?

It all happened so fast, the huge explosions, the ground shaking, bullets flying. I lost track of the others. We all ran in separate directions. I ran and tripped. Voices shouting, more gunfire, then a hand, a big hand on my shoulder and I looked up at a face I had never seen before, but a face I would never, ever forget.

Chapter 16

Nopi

I saw only big men running in all directions. The ground shook again. Lucky! Nowhere. Lights, grenades . . . the battle raged all around me. I looked for some place that didn't have men and guns pointing out of it and saw an empty clearing to the right. I ran as fast as I could. I watched my feet and jumped over a stream.

"Where are you running to, little sister?" I looked up and saw no one. What was this voice inside my head?

I veered to the right and ran straight into a rebel soldier. His clothes hung on him in pieces, one sleeve ripped off. He grabbed me and I watched his face laugh, while his eyes remained cold.

Lucky

I have the face memorized, the face of the man who captured me, the man who protected me and taught me everything I know. The first time I saw this man, when he grabbed me in the forest, his huge hand bigger than my face, he grabbed my shirt and said, "Boy, you're just the fresh meat we were looking for. Come on, get to your feet. Frog! I've got a live one!"

The man who found me is my C.O. His name is Peanut Butter. He's a famous officer in the government forces. Frog is his right-hand man. Frog brought me and some other boys they found during that battle back to their main camp, a field of tents, too many to count.

That first night they gave me something to eat, but the next day they only gave me maggot-filled rice. "Can't waste good food on animals," Frog said.

During basic training they told me I am nothing. I am scum. I am worse than shit. I have to beg for food and water, and carry heavy things like I used to for Sergeant Saint.

I make up poems or songs and say them over and over again in my head to keep from falling down in the mud and giving up.

Alone in this world.

No one but me.

Wish I could see.

Wish I were free.

How long would I be there? I wondered. Who could I trust? I knew no one. I didn't even know how to speak the language Frog and Peanut Butter and some of the other soldiers spoke. Would the war end soon like the last one did?

Should I plan an escape? I wasn't the only one thinking these thoughts. A few nights later some of the big boys almost got away, but they were dragged in front of the rest of us and cut up so bad they fainted. The soldiers made sure the boys didn't die though. We had to leave them in the jungle with ants all over them when we marched on.

"No one leaves here. No one, you hear?" Peanut Butter loomed over us and spit came flying out of his mouth. "And if you even think about it, I'll know because I read minds. I'll make you kill each other. I'll make you kill the weak. So be strong because it's better to live than to die. And the only way you'll live in my army is if you obey everything we order you! What are you staring at?"

He made us pray to him, and ask for guns. We small boys knelt down in the mud and chanted, "Give us guns! Give us guns!"

Chapter 17

Lucky

I wonder if you can see the way we look. I will tell you.

We are Peanut Butter's Small Boy Unit. He keeps promising us guns, and he tells us when we get to go into battle and become fighters, no bullets will touch us. I don't believe him, but other boys say it's true, that the soldiers can give us special pills that keep us safe and make our skin bulletproof.

I watch the C.O. all the time. His nose is broad and flat. He looks much different than most people I've seen — taller, with wide shoulders. That's the funny thing about Liberia. We come from different tribes, but five percent of the population is descended from ex-slaves who came back to Africa from America and the Caribbean. And those people don't look like anything at all, not even West African. They might have the high cheekbones of a Somali, or the nose of an Ethiopian.

These ex-slaves came back to Africa in the 1800s and then turned around and made the people already living in Liberia into slaves. It wasn't until 1951 that all Liberians could vote. But even then it wasn't really a free election. This is all stuff Peanut Butter told us at night around the fire.

One day Peanut Butter finally gave us our guns. It was

after we won a battle. He ordered some of us to run into the forest toward the enemy and scream as loud as we could to drive them out into the open. It worked, so Peanut Butter was happy with us. We each got our own AK-47. I took such good care of mine, it shone. I took it apart and cleaned it every night. I cradled it in my arms like a baby.

My AK.

Baby and me.

I braid my hair the same as the other members of the Small Boy Unit. We wear sunglasses, even at night. Peanut Butter says they make him see better in the dark.

Chapter 18

Nopi

I am one wife of three belonging to a colonel in the rebel forces. He chose me and he trained me to shoot at targets and hit them. He likes to send me into battle and tell the others his third wife is the best one yet because she can go into the middle of the fighting and doesn't even flinch at the explosions.

I don't believe him. I don't love him. I would have run away the very first night, but his second wife, a girl younger than me, her name is Innocence, told me he would cut off my arms if they caught me. She said she needed my help because she would be having her baby soon. So I stayed for her. And I stayed for her baby. But after the baby was born, I have dreamed about running away every single night.

I don't care what he says. I don't care if he kills me. I don't care. I asked Innocence to distract him tonight. So I'm running away.

It's been too long. I don't even know how many months — or is it a year? No time out here in the jungle. Where to go? Run!

A lot of nights I'm hiding in the bush. I even climb

trees to sleep in them. I stay away from the camps, stay off the trails, but I'm smart. There's a river, and I know the rivers empty into the ocean. So I travel at night to avoid the soldiers. During the day I cover myself with leaves and burrow halfway underground so no one will see me. And I sleep while ants crawl on my legs. The river is my friend. She is wide and free and all I have to do is go where she goes.

I'm eating wild bananas. The ground is muddy. My river goes faster and faster — I can tell because of the twigs I throw into the water; they get swept up and disappear faster than I can run. All this in the moonlight. Too many moons. What am I doing? Where am I going?

I run away and find the ocean. My river brings me to a beach. I wander up and down the beach. There's a group of people and a small boat.

"Please, can I come with you?" I beg them. I don't tell them the soldiers might be after me. I don't want to scare them any worse. I don't hear yes and I don't hear no, but I climb into the boat and take one of the toddlers whose mother has her hands full with a baby. I take this little boy onto my lap and smell his hair and think about Lucky.

Where is he?

Chapter 19

Lucky

In one of the towns we attacked I found a book in a school and picked it up off the floor. I carried this book around with me everywhere. I stuck it into my shorts and carried it beside my skin. I liked the pictures and made up a story to go with them. I tell some of the other boys this story over and over again until we all have it memorized. When the war is over, I'll learn more than just the alphabet. I'll learn how to read. I had a dream to be a soccer player and make loads of money and listen to the crowds cheering me on as I travel the world. But it wasn't a dream of the heart. My dream now is to go back to school. It's all I want. If I go back to school, I can read books.

They hand out pills, blue- and red-colored capsules with white powder inside. "This is magic medicine. Swallow the pills and no bullet can kill you." Most of the kids in the Small Boy Unit believe this story. After all, we're all still alive, aren't we?

Another thing Peanut Butter does is talk about blood, and drinking the blood of his enemies so we get more courage like lions do. I saw him do this, we all did, and it made me throw up, which meant I didn't get any food for three days.

They beat us, and yell at us all the time. There is no honor for the Small Boy Unit. I'm just glad they don't call us less than shit anymore.

What do you dream of? To run away? I did once. I dreamed of running back to when I was a small, small child, but I don't dream that now. Not me. Where would we go? Who'll take us back after what we've done? Here we have food and water and favor because of the C.O. I have no home to run back to, no past, no present, no future.

Run away? If I try to leave, they force me to stay. Who am I in this place? Lucky to be alive, the C.O. says. I know I'm changing. I want different things now. They may treat me like a slave, but I still dream. Who do I want to be?

When we were little, my sister and I were in class together when the teacher asked us what our dreams were. I didn't know then, so I said what came into the hearts and mouths of all the other little boys — a soccer star. My sister said she wanted to be president. Everyone laughed at her, but I didn't.

I wonder if she'll ever hear again.

"What's your real name?" the C.O. asked me. My name is Lucky. My sister's name is New Policy, but we call her Nopi for short. Everyone has different nicknames here. Lucky? I guess you could say our parents liked to think positively.

Now my commander calls me Peanut Butter II, but all of us in the Small Boy Unit are called Peanut Butter II after him. Later, I just told people my name was Lucky because I was still alive. My sister knew my name. She used to call me Go-go because I never stopped dancing. But the name my mother and father gave me — this I've lost. How'll I know it's me they're searching for if I no longer see their faces or know the name they call out in the dark? Who am I really?

Nothing but a small boy, lost in the forest.

Chapter 20

Nopi

The ocean goes on and on in every direction. The man in charge has lost the rudder in a storm. We have no oars. We go up and down, up and down with the waves. I've thrown up so often there's nothing left. Who will rescue us? Where are we? The land is nowhere to be seen. We are all too tired and thirsty to be angry. I see no one I recognize. This little boy in my lap, his eyes are beautiful and round. He calls me sister. I call him little brother.

A giant ship approaches. We stand and wave, the boat threatens to turn over. There are too many of us. I don't know how to swim and the waves frighten me. "Have mercy!" I shout with the others. And then I fall and blessed black takes me into its arms.

Chapter 21

Lucky

Politicians lie.

Generals lie.

My father is a gun.

My god is a gun. That's what Peanut Butter told me. He said I had to listen to the voice of my gun like I would listen to the voice of God. When it thunders, I'd better jump. And me and my gun, we can make people become neighbors of God by sending them to heaven. He'd put his face down in front of mine and sneer, "Who's your daddy?"

Me, I'm the son of a gun.

In this mud everywhere I dream of being dry. I dream of a big plate of rice and meat. I dream of watching football on TV. I dream of being able to read. I dream of my sister hearing me. I dream of finding my parents.

"We, the army, we are your family now." Peanut Butter's words make me think about my mother and father. Where are they? Did they escape the soldiers? Are they looking for Nopi and me? Every day hunger and thirst wait for me as I build up my career of walking. All alone. Don't want to leave anymore.

Nowhere to go.
So slow.
Blow by blow.
Don't want to be eaten by no crow.

Chapter 22

Nopi

When I wake it's onshore. Oh, I am so happy to have my face in the sand. I am alone. Where is everyone? Where's the great ship? I look for the toddler on my lap. Everyone is gone. Did we die?

I crawl farther from the surf. Is this a dream? I see ripened plantains and eat them raw. I find water in a nearby creek and drink. I wander down the road and join a group of people. They are eating crab they found on the beach and share it with me.

"Where are you from?" I ask, watching their faces.

"We're refugees. We've left everything."

"What is this place?"

"This is a refugee camp."

I have nowhere else to go, so I follow them to a place where a European man is handing out bowls of rice and cooking oil. I climb a hill and see fields with endless rows of blue tents.

I ask the man at the desk if my parents are here. "Are there other refugee camps for Liberians?" He looks like he wants to laugh and I can't read his lips. I ask, "What? I can't hear well." There. I've said the words.

His mouth makes the shapes. "Yeah. Try Ivory Coast, Guinea, Ghana, and Nigeria. You Liberians are all over the world."

There are advantages to being a refugee. You see the world and you learn foreign languages. At least those who hear can. When I left this first camp and had to walk for weeks until we reached safety in the Ivory Coast, the people I traveled with learned French there.

As I watch the lips of those speaking French, I know nothing of what is being said.

Everywhere I go I look for the photos of Lucky and my parents on the walls where you enter. How can there be so many faces of missing people, and none of them are mine?

I still carry around Grandma's cane. It helped me beat a man who was attacking another girl I traveled with. One night I tried to take it apart, thinking there might be diamonds hidden inside. But it was just a hollow shell.

Chapter 23

Lucky

Son of a gun.

On the run.

No way it's fun.

You wouldn't know 'til you're the one.

In the days when I wanted to escape I couldn't because I was afraid of being caught again. Man, you should see what they do to you here if you try to run away. The worst part is being the one who does the doing.

So many nights are just a blur. But I remember this one night like it happened a few hours ago. I'm supposed to be keeping watch, right? We're near the front line, so I'm not the only one. I walk back and forth on my stretch of forest, between two groups of trees, when I hear my name.

"Lucky! Is that you, Lucky?"

I peer toward the sound. Who's that? Who's calling me by my old name? Even more important, whose voice is coming out of the part of the forest where the enemy is supposed to be?

I cock my AK and look behind me. No one around, so I get down and jungle crawl toward the enemy camp. The closer I get, the louder I can hear all their voices.

"Yo."

"It's me," comes the voice from under a tree just to my right, in the shadow of the moon.

"Me, who?"

"James."

This didn't fit. I had been with the Small Boy Unit so long, I couldn't find that part of me that used to know James. But that part of me wanted to be found because next thing you know, I'm saying, "James?" and standing up and running toward that tree and dropping my gun and giving this guy who's taller than me a huge hug. Man, the tears are even going down my cheeks.

I can see by the moonlight that he's really different. He wears a motorcycle helmet. When he takes it off, I see his hair is all braided long.

"You're with the rebels?"

"Yeah, man. That's my people."

So now I figure out that clans that used to be friends, that used to intermarry, have become enemies. That's what they mean by ethnic differences. I don't learn that term until after the war. But right now, with my friend's voice all over me and his face lit by the moon, I can't get enough of what he's saying.

Seeing James wakes up all sorts of longing for home and my parents and seeing my sister and my grandma's cooking.

We spend the night talking, whispering the whole time so neither of our sentries will hear us. "What's the worst thing you've done?" he asks me.

I don't want to answer. But it's James, so I do. "They made me kill this little boy who couldn't walk anymore, he was so tired and thirsty." I don't tell him about standing up and charging with the rest of my unit into a wall of rebel soldiers and shooting and hacking at them with my cutlass. It's what I'm trained to do. I'm a killing machine, that's what Peanut Butter keeps telling us. But that's war. That was the enemy. Killing that little boy is the thing that keeps me awake at night.

James tells me his worst story. I'm trying hard not to listen because it makes my heart stop and go.

"I can't tell you what happened then, it's too . . ." He stops talking and swallows hard.

I close my eyes tight. "Man."

"Yeah."

I hear a whistle. "That from your side or mine?" I ask.

"Mine." James stands up. I do, too, and we shake hands and hug.

"Take care, man," I say.

"Yeah."

Part 4

Chapter 24

Lucky

Where am I? What do I do now? I want to eat. I'm so thirsty I drink things you don't want to know about.

I am just a child.

When do I get a break? I don't mean to sound like I'm feeling sorry for myself, but why me? I've spent my walking career dreaming of going back to school. We were just learning how to read when the war started. That book I found — I still carry it with me wherever I go. The words are faded, but I've made up a story. That story isn't mine, though. It's the story of the child I wanted to be.

The child I wanted to be — could that be you? Maybe if the story I made up is not my story, it might be yours. You live in a place of peace? I remember complaining to my parents about the food they served me. And don't think I didn't want more things. Hey, we're more alike than you think. But that stuff I complained about, now I wish instead I had just realized how good I had it. Next time I drink water and it's clean, or sit bored in school, next time I wish I didn't have so many chores to do, or whenever I dream of becoming a soccer player or president, then I will think of others, others having it bad — like I did, and my sister.

If there is a next time.

I was made to do the things I did. I swear it. If I think of them now, it kills me inside. Do you have that too? Feeling so bad? When we fought in Monrovia I saw our home, burned and looted. I went back a second time and it looked like it had caught fire again. Now the walls were all that was left standing; the roof had burned right off.

Each day blends into the next. I no longer want to run away. I want to fight well. Yes, I was forced to kill, but I've chosen to stay. The army, this regiment, these other boys, they are my family now.

The gun is my god.

This is the way I lived, the way I thought and fought for five long years. When those five years were over and another peace caught up with us, this time it was different because the U.N. sent soldiers to make sure we didn't rush ahead into war again.

Then I found myself turning in my AK to that Irishman. I was crazy. Crazy mad. Man, you know what it feels like for a soldier to surrender? Everything you've been holding onto for dear life just gets stripped right off you, like it was skin or something. And that's exactly how it felt when I gave my gun up, like I was a snake who'd just shed its skin but had nothing new to protect me so I would get killed soon. I was crazy mad because I was afraid.

After five years of believing I was something, I found out I'm nothing. Nothing but a little cloud of dust, like the one my rifle sent up when it landed on top of that weapons pile. Turning in my AK meant surrendering everything

I had just spent the last five years believing in: the gun as my god, my whole way of life. Letting go of my gun meant letting go of everything I had been taught to think was most important — the killing, the battles, the orders. None of it mattered. It was nothing. I was nothing. What had all that fighting been for? Yeah, I was mad. Besides, the world had let me down. Where was everybody during those five years? How come no grown-ups could find me?

If you ask me, those five years can't be counted. The memories blur together. Strange that I can remember Sergeant Saint and what happened in those few months when I was younger better than the things that happened for years when I was older. I think of Sergeant Saint more vividly than what goes on now. I guess sometimes you just don't want to remember.

I spent five years fighting for Peanut Butter.

The war came and went. I didn't even know it was five years until it was over. The war ended a year ago. Now I'm sixteen. Man, I fought from ages ten to fifteen. That's what I did. Different battles, different promises from the politicians. Different men in power stealing diamonds and lying to the people. But I kept fighting, as I was told. I did well and they rewarded me, paid me well, made me someone important who the other boys looked up to.

People think we're not children anymore. But we still laugh. I still play soccer. Now that the war is over, some of the guys from the Small Boy Unit and I have gotten together a soccer team here in Monrovia.

Nopi

I can tell you how it happened. Three or four times I got the news that the war was over. I started heading for Monrovia, together with other refugees heading home. Then another war would break out. We call them World Wars 1, 2, and 3.

Finally the day came when I found the old ruins of our house. I stayed there, praying World War 4 wouldn't happen. I begged for food and stole from the garbage of others.

I looked up one day and saw both my parents running toward me. I didn't hear their voices, but I could see their smiles and hear their laughter in my heart.

A few weeks later Lucky found us.

Lucky

The third time I came home even the walls no longer stood. Our home was nothing but a pile of old mud bricks. But next to it rose one new wall. I saw that wall and knew my family was somewhere nearby. I waited and in the evening I looked toward the setting sun. It was right in my eyes when I heard my name. I heard them call my name, "Lucky! Lucky!" I started running and found myself in my mother's arms. Our grandma was dead, but Pa was there, and so was Nopi. How come when so many had lost all their families, I still got to keep mine?

Nopi

I know the kind of food Lucky likes — fufu with chicken and a nice hot spicy palava sauce, pepper soup, cassava leaves, and potato greens. I've made it for him tonight, a big plate of rice and meat, just the way he likes it. He's going to school now, learning how to read. And me? I've got an appointment on board a Mercy ship, a hospital ship that entered port last month. They want to operate on my ear! They say it might just be blood that's blocking my hearing.

When I'm cooking, I miss Grandma.

Chapter 25

Lucky

James came to Monrovia and found me.

"Hey, man," he said. He was waiting for me under a tree, just like before. Only now there were no other soldiers around us. He'd cut off his hair and wore it short now, like we all did. That way you can't tell by looking who was on which side of the war. If you know a man's last name, you could tell which ethnic group he belongs to, though. James' name had him pegged as an ex-rebel. I thought all this while I watched him standing there. He wouldn't stop looking over his shoulder. I wondered if I did the same.

"You get the money from the U.N.?" he asked.

I nodded.

"I know how you can get more," James said. "The Ivory Coast armies are offering four hundred dollars a month to go fight in their war."

"But you turned in your gun."

"Got another."

"Don't do it, man." My counselor says to the boys who want to go to Ivory Coast that the path of peace leads to life, and the path of revenge leads to death. Our group sits around with her, telling stories. It's easy to find comfort in the horror stories of others when they're worse than your own. I'm wondering what my counselor would say to James right now.

"Don't do it, man. If you don't want to die, don't do it. You can become part of our family."

"No way. I'm going to be a fighter forever," James said.

When James walked away I watched him until I couldn't see him anymore. Then I stooped down and drew in the dust, losing track of time as if it were my friend.

Nopi

I watch the ocean waves crash on the beach and remember that booming sound. I see the palm fronds pushed back and forth, up and down by the breeze, and I hope soon now I will hear them rustle.

After so many years away from Liberia, I love this place even more, my homeland. There will be elections soon..The U.N. soldiers are everywhere. The Irish and the Swedish are the crack troops. A woman is running for president. I'm going to vote for her. I can now, since I'm eighteen. And I'm going back to school.

This is my story. It's who I am. My little brother protected me when he was just a small boy.

I'm alive by the grace of God. That part of me that wandered from place to place and had to be a wife, she's died and gone to heaven. We're starting over here.

Lucky

I wrote this story down for a friend. First I had to learn how to read and write. That took a while. You know that old book I carried around all those years? By the time I knew how to read, the letters printed on the pages had faded so much I couldn't tell what the story was. You think it was fun sitting in a classroom with kids who were seven? Me, a man, a fighter?

Yeah, I turned in my gun and went to school. They asked us to tell our stories. Couldn't then, but had to now that I can write. It's hard, going back to hear the children's voices. My best memories are the ones from when I was just a small, small boy.

There's a lot of talk now about forgiveness. Can't forgive myself for what was bad. Part of me is bad and selfish and wants to hang out with the bad kids, and part of me wants to be good. We're supposed to forgive our enemies so there will be lasting peace. I'm supposed to forgive my parents for not finding me. I have to forgive my friend James, who became my enemy. But what about forgiving myself? For Nopi getting beaten so hard she went deaf. For them coming to take my parents away and do God knows what to them for diamonds. For all the bad stuff that happened. Yeah, I was forced to kill others. No way I'll ever be welcome back in any of the villages we attacked. I don't think my parents even want to know what I've done, and I'm not going to tell them. Why would I? I want to be loved.

They have us going to school now. I heard some of the schools have nothing but rocks for the kids to sit on.

I watched Nopi weave an orange scarf through her hair this morning.

The United Nations came. I hope they stick around. They gave me money for my gun, but I gave it all to Ma. She touched my face and called me by my real name. Isaac. She told me my name means "Laughter."

But I think it might be better to just keep my nickname. When the counselor asked, I told her my name was Lucky. I'm the one still alive. I'm the lucky one.

Who are these children in this story? Me and my sister.

The counselor tells us that our stories are more precious than the largest diamond in the world, and that's the worth of one child. How come I don't feel worth so much? What am I worth?

That's what I thought about as I wrote this story for my friend.

I've written this down here for you, James. Wherever you are.

Remember me.

Author's Note

Can you imagine it? Children walking around with weapons? Children who are forced to hurt other children, children who are forced to defend their country? In Liberia many children had to do just that during the civil war.

This story is meant to open a door and let you see a part of the world most people will never see. Running water, a toilet, and going to school might be normal parts of your life — maybe you don't even notice them — but how do the children in this story talk about these things? Try to put yourself in the shoes of the characters. Imagine that this was your sister, your brother, or you. Are there more differences or more similarities? This story takes place in Liberia, but it's about children just like you.

A typical Liberian idea is to "make palava," which means to gather in a circle under some trees and argue and discuss until an agreement is reached. This attitude is one of the contributing factors to the current peace. It's held together by the hopes of young people I met and talked to, former child soldiers who spent years being forced to live a nightmare while still daring to dream. They dreamed of peace and they dreamed of school. Now, these dreams are coming true.

Parts of this story are a little hard to read. These parts

were hard to write, too! I still hear the actual voices of the young people who told me these things. Everything described in this story really did happen.

War is always terrible, but civil war is the worst kind of war. It's when neighbors and in-laws and friends become enemies because government leaders are greedy for power and money. So they lie and break their promises. How would you feel if your neighbor suddenly showed up at your door with a gun in his hand and stole everything that belongs to you and your parents? That's what happens in civil wars.

Some people say children should be protected from the truth when it is painful. But civil wars and other terrible things do happen in the world. There are dark places all around us, not just in war-torn countries. Other dark places are when bad things happen like death and divorce and pain. But it is in these dark places that we see how bright the gift of hope shines. Children are the world's future. If your heart is touched by the hearts of the children in this story, I hope you will help bring a wiser future to the world. Hope is what I found in Liberia. Hope against all odds, as people — and especially children — dared to let go of the past and face a future with nothing but their dreams. What are your dreams?

— Anne de Graaf
www.annedegraaf.com

Anne de Graaf at a school in Dekegar.

Liberia — Facts and Figures

General Information

• On the maps below, you can see where Liberia is located.

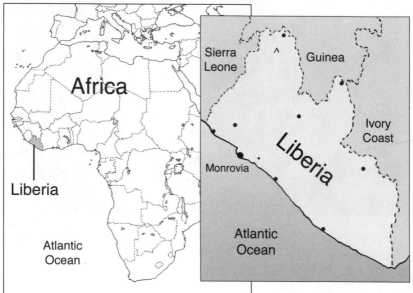

• Liberia has a population of 3.8 million people. The capital of Liberia is the coastal city of Monrovia. Liberia has an area of 43,000 square miles.

• The people speak many languages: English and 29 different African languages.

- In Liberia there are Christians, Muslims, and believers in traditional African religions.
- The average life expectancy is not high. Men die on average by the time they are 56, and women by the time they are 59 years old.
- The currency is the Liberian dollar. Its symbol is L$.
- Liberia exports diamonds, iron, rubber, wood, coffee, and cacao.
- The national income per person is $200 per year.

Weather and Natural Setting

Liberia is about the size of the state of Tennessee and lies on the west coast of Africa. It has an extensive coast and inland rises to a maximum altitude of about 1,000 meters, or 3,280 feet. Tropical forest covers most of the country. Low mountains rise in the northeast. A dust-laden wind called the *harmattan* blows from the Sahara Desert from December to March.

It is a land criss-crossed by rivers watering fertile soil that supports rubber, palm oil, and tropical fruit plantations. Liberia has rich timber resources and its mountains bear high-quality iron ore. Liberia's natural resources also include significant deposits of diamonds and gold.

From October to March, during the period of low sun, the weather is generally dry with many hot, sunny days. The season of high sun, from April to September, is the rainy season. The rainfall increases to a peak in July and August and then decreases until rain has almost ceased by November.

The average temperature is between 72 and 95 degrees Fahrenheit.

The water supply in Monrovia.

Food

The staple diet consists of rice, fish, and vegetables. While Liberians also eat cassava (a type of root) and its by-products, dumboy and fufu, rice is king in Liberia. It was the increase in the price of rice in 1980 that ignited the rice riots, which subsequently lead to the military coup of 1980. Liberians eat their food hot and spicy. Cayenne pepper and other hot peppers are always added to Liberian dishes.

Many types of greens and vegetables are eaten in Liberia, including cassava leaves. Potato greens, which come from the leaves of potatoes, taste just like spinach. They are usually fried with onions, peppers, beef, or chicken. In western countries potato greens are often thrown away or used as cattle feed.

Popcorn seller.

Daily Life

Most Liberians eat one meal a day. For over ten years there has been no electricity, except for that made by individual generators. Tens and thousands of teenagers have never even seen an electric light. And there is no running water. So every day a great deal of time and energy goes into getting water for cooking and cleaning, and doing by hand all the things that might be done with the help of machines and electricity in more developed countries. This includes gathering fuel for fires so the meals can be cooked.

Over 85% of adults are out of work and try to make a living as best they can. Sometimes this means buying things in the country, like charcoal, wood, or food, and walking into the city to sell it at roadside stands or to people in cars. Many times the only way of transporting goods is by walking and carrying it on one's head, or by pushing a wheelbarrow.

Almost 80% of the population lives on less than $1 per day. This is all they have to spend on food, drinks, and clothing. Three-quarters of the Liberian population has no access to safe drinking water and only one out of ten have access to medical care. One out of every eight people is at risk for AIDS.

A shop in Monrovia.

Challenges for the Liberian government and its people include reconnecting water and electricity, improving rural sanitation, getting buses on roads, halting the exodus of teachers to organizations that pay them more, and re-plastering pockmarked buildings.

Primary Education

In Liberia half of all adult men and 80% of the women cannot read. Almost all children 15 and under cannot read because they grew up during the 14-year-long war, when most schools were shut down. This means teenagers now sit alongside 6-year-olds in the schools.

According to the Liberian constitution, all children have a right to attend school. In reality, though, many Liberian children cannot go to school because they must pay school fees and pay for their books and uniforms. It costs about $100 per year for a 10-year-old to attend school in Liberia. This is as much as the average Liberian makes in an entire year. Even if they can come up with the money for school, there are still many areas in Liberia where there just are no schools. They were destroyed during the war and have not been rebuilt.

In some places, because the teachers are the only ones who know how to read, they have been hired to work for government or aid agencies, so there are no teachers. Other schools have nothing but rocks for the children to sit upon — no pens or slates or chalk or books. So the children learn by drawing in the dust.

This is a good school — there are benches, books, and pens.

The school system in Liberia is similar to America's: after grade school comes high school, then university education. All levels of school are in desperate need of teachers and supplies.

History

1800-2003

Liberia was founded in the mid-1800s by freed American and Caribbean slaves. They, in turn, enslaved the people already living in the area. They set up huge plantations modeled after the plantations where they had worked as slaves. The former slaves' descendants make up 5% of the current population.

Liberia is Africa's oldest republic, but all through the 1990s it became better known for its long and bloody civil war, and its role in helping fuel the war in neighboring Sierra Leone.

The West African nation was relatively calm until 1980 when riots broke out over the price of rice. The government was overthrown by the army led by Sergeant Samuel Doe. This marked the end of leadership by the minority descendants of the former slaves. These Americo-Liberians, as they were called, had ruled since independence in 1847. But it also marked the beginning of a long period of instability.

In the late 1980s, civil war broke out when Charles Taylor's militia overran much of the countryside. He took over Monrovia, the capital, in 1990. Samuel Doe was executed. Fighting intensified as the rebels split into different groups and fought each other, the Liberian government forces, and West African peacekeepers. Since 1995 several peace agreements have been signed. In 1997 Charles Taylor was elected as president.

Unfortunately, the brief period of peace soon ended when anti-government fighting broke out and Mr. Taylor accused the neighboring country of Guinea of supporting the rebellion. Meanwhile Ghana, Nigeria, and others accused Mr. Taylor of backing rebels in Sierra Leone.

Since 2003

Matters came to a head in 2003. President Taylor came under increasing pressure by the rebel armies and the international community to resign. He stepped down and went into exile in Nigeria. The United Nations (U.N.) brought in 15,000 troops from all over the world to keep the peace.

In October 2004 riots in Monrovia left 16 people dead. In June 2005 the U.N. extended a ban on diamond exports. For years the sale of Liberian diamonds had paid for weapons and ammunition for the war. Now that was no longer possible. In September 2005 Liberia agreed that the international community should supervise its finances in an effort to counter corruption. A transitional government steered the country toward elections, and in November 2005 Liberians voted, free of violence or intimidation for the very first time in the history of their country.

On November 23, 2005, Ellen Johnson-Sirleaf became the first woman to be elected as an African head of state. She took office in January 2006. Early that year a Truth and

Reconciliation Commission was set up to investigate human rights abuses between 1979 and 2003. In the spring of 2006 the former Liberian president, Charles Taylor, appeared before a U.N.-backed court in Sierra Leone on charges of crimes against humanity. The trial was moved to The Hague, The Netherlands for safety reasons.

U.N. troops, consisting of more than 15,000 young soldiers from countries around the world. They guard the peace in Liberia and the people treat them as heroes.

This is an election poster from 2005.

This is the front page of a Liberian newspaper. Notice the article at the bottom that declares the victory of Ellen Johnson-Sirleaf to be certain.

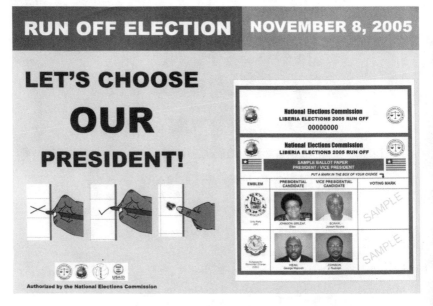

Another election poster. On the poster you can see a picture of the election ballot, with instructions about how to fill it out.

War

The 14-year-long war covered all parts of Liberia. Around 250,000 people were killed in Liberia's civil war and many thousands more fled the fighting. The conflict left the country in economic ruin and overrun with weapons.

The U.N. maintains some 15,000 soldiers in Liberia from countries all over the world. It is one of the organization's most expensive peacekeeping operations.

More than 100,600 young people in Liberia used to be child soldiers and are now trying to put together the pieces of their lives after the war. At employment agencies in Monrovia, young men line up waiting for job offers. The only skills they know are how to clean and repair guns. They cannot earn a living unless they learn a trade.

Child Soldiers

There are over 300,000 child soldiers all over the world. Children are often kidnapped, sometimes even from refugee camps, and forced to fight in armies and militias. These children don't want to fight, but they have no choice. They are given a gun and are abused and forced to kill people. They are told that bullets cannot hurt them if they take certain drugs. Often they have no family anymore since the army that kidnapped them has attacked the village where they used to live. The villagers are either dead or have fled. Now the army is their family.

The AK-47 rifle is so lightweight that a child can carry it and shoot with it. An AK-47 costs the same as one chicken.

Many child soldiers have never been to school or could not finish school, and cannot read or write. They have learned no skills that would help them to get jobs. All they know is how to be a soldier.

The U.N. encourages former child soldiers to turn in their guns and participate in training that will help them to learn a trade and earn a living.

Photo by the author of a DDRR t-shirt, worn by former child soldiers who have gone through the Disarmament Demobilization Reintegration Resocialization program offered by the U.N. to former combatants who turn in their weapons. They receive cash and trauma therapy, and are taught a trade.

It is very difficult for child soldiers to rebuild their lives. James Singbah, a former child soldier in Liberia, has written how he sees life now. His life was ruined by the war.

A Poem about My Life until the War Damaged My Life

Oh, my life. I have no hope.
Oh, my life — my father and mother are dead.
Oh, my life — a great setback to my future.
Oh, my life — will I ever feel as a human among my
friends and schoolmates?
Oh, my life — the war has damaged my life.
Oh, my life is my enemy.

Not all children and teenagers who have been soldiers are hopeless. Despite the terrible things they have seen and done, they still dream about the future.

Read about the dream Stephen T. Fallah has for his future.

My Dream of My Future

If I finish my Education, I want to earn degree in Science. I want to become a Scientist, and I wish to go abroad to do my studies in Science, Mathematics and English. My major subject will be Science, while the others will be minor.

I hope to become a better person in my future so that I can help to develop my country by bringing in some Scientific materials, building industries, schools, hospitals, and bringing electricity, etc. All these plans can come through education. If I am blessed to go further with my education, I will also be the same blessing to my country Liberia.

There are also former child soldiers who have written poems about their future. Anne de Graaf met Chupee Wee-Wee Gaines in Liberia. Chupee told her life story to Anne. During the war her father hid her in a closet for a week, so that the soldiers living in her house would not find her. Chupee was thirteen years old then. She wrote this poem:

Love
The world and everything in it come alive
When just a few things are said and done.
How would it be without these letters?
Will there ever be smiling faces?
Will someone ever have a second chance?
The world can stand still, but with it things and people evolve.

— Chupee WeeWee Gaines

Drawings By The Children

These drawings were made by children in a refugee camp during a creativity workshop organized by Save the Children.

I Hear that Troops Have Arrived
Yea!!! More Troops are Still coming
UN say, COME and learn so You Can get this, CERTIFICAT
Certificate
UN
UN
We want Peace
Iam learning my Trade
12345
54321
I am learning Computer trad
Wilson Corner Children Development Club
Thomas Siaffa

° After you disarm go for checkup
and get medicine

The doctor checking
disarm Fighters
and giving
them medicine

Wilson CORNER children

Development Club

We Want
Peace

UN

UN

UN Truck carrying disarm
Fighters to caretaker camp

A hand-drawn comic strip of what it is like to turn in your gun to the U.N. at the end of the war.

Aid Organizations That Contributed to This Book

ZOA Refugee Care
www.zoa.nl

Woord en Daad
www.woordendaad.nl

Tearfund
www.tearfund.org

Sources for the facts and figures in this book include websites by the BBC, CIA, and Dutch Ministry of Foreign Affairs.

Acknowledgments

I would like to thank the following people for their contribution to this book (in alphabetical order):

Thomas Baryee, Michael Clements, Lucky Glen Clerk (Lucky Boy), Cecilia T.M. Danuwelo, Monroe B. Dean, Rosa Dillon, Erik de Graaf, Boima Fahnbulleh, Onike Gooding Freeman, Chuka Tutu Gaines, Chupee WeeWee Gaines, Flomo V. Golanyon, Wietse Groenveld, Robin Jones Gunn, Robert C. Hedley and Sonja Hedley, Robert Jallah, Martin G. Karnwhine, Yenneh Kasselie, Olu Arthur King, Alfred S. Kpannah, D. Maxim Kumeh, Bai Kiazo Lu-Fao, Stephen NC'ube, George Otieno Oloo, Franklin Philips, Mambu Quoi and Anneke Quoi-de Kok, Earl Reeves, Joshua V. Robinson, Sr., Edwin Slocum, Corine Verdoold, Urey Walters, H. Phoebe Waritay, Aukelien Wierenga, and E. Sonie Zubah; and Nopi and her brother, two children who flew with me from Monrovia to Brussels and now live in Philadelphia, Pennsylvania.

I would also like to thank the following organizations:

Don Boscoe Homes
Save the Children Community Resource Center
(for the drawings by Liberian children in refugee camps,
including Konneh camp in Kakata)
WANEP-Liberia (West Africa Network for Peace)
WIPNET (Women in Peacebuilding Network)
ZOA Refugee Care

— Anne de Graaf

Questions for discussion:

1. Nopi says in chapter 1 that she and her brother are not much different from you. Do you think this is true? In what ways can you see that you are like Nopi and Lucky?

2. Lucky says that before the soldiers came he had a dream to be a star soccer player. Do you have a dream about something you want in the future? How does Lucky's dream change after his experience in the war?

3. Lucky's best friend James is from another tribe. Before the war comes to their village, this is not a problem. How does the war change their relationship?

4. Nopi and Lucky end up harming others during the war even though they do not know what they are fighting for or against. Why do they take the guns and use them? Do you think they are guilty because of their actions, or are they victims? Explain your answer.

5. Lucky says he is crazy for giving up his gun to the United Nations. Why does he feel this way? Why does he decide to give up his gun anyway? Unlike Lucky, James decides to join another army in the Ivory Coast after the war ends in Liberia. Why does he make this decision?

6. What painful feelings about himself does Lucky have after the war ends? What helps Lucky cope with these troubling feelings and memories? What does Nopi feel she has lost because of her experience in the war?

7. Lucky's counselor encourages him to tell his story as a way to heal from his painful past. How can storytelling be a helpful way to deal with your feelings?

8. Using online resources, find more information on child soldiers. Which other countries have children participating in armed conflict? Who do you think is responsible for taking action against the use of children in armed conflict?